Snakes legs and cows eggs

Seriously Silly Stories

by

Adam Bushnell

Illustrated by Vince Reid

First Published
April 07 in Great Britain by

PUBLISHING

ISBN-10: 1-905637-21-7
ISBN-13: 978-1-905637-21-8

Educational Printing Services Limited
Albion Mill, Water Street, Great Harwood, Blackburn BB6 7QR
Telephone: (01254) 882080   Fax: (01254) 882010
E-mail: enquiries@eprint.co.uk   Website: www.eprint.co.uk

Contents

To
Tracy and Michael

1: Anansi the Storyteller
(Caribbean)

Tiger was the king of the forest. In the evening he would sit with his nose high up in the air and all of the animals would gather in a circle around him. They talked and they laughed together.

"Who is the strongest of us all?" the bullfrog would croak.

"Tiger! Tiger! Tiger!" all the animals would say.

"And who is the weakest of us all?" the bullfrog would croak.

"Anansi! Anansi! Anansi!" all the animals would laugh.

But one day Anansi came down from his web and crawled across the forest floor until he got to the circle of animals.

Anansi crept up to Tiger and said, "Tiger, you are so strong and mighty. Please grant me one favour."

Tiger held his nose high up in the air, closed his eyes and answered slowly, "What is it you want Anansi?"

"We all know you are the strongest of us all. This is why we give your name to many

things like Tiger stories, Tiger moths, Tiger lilies, Tiger this and Tiger that. I would like to have something named after me."

Tiger regarded his claws and said, "What is it that you want?"

"The stories," said Anansi, "I want the stories to be named after me."

Tiger liked the stories but instead of just saying no he decided to play a trick on Anansi.

"Very well, if you can catch Mr Snake alive, then I will give you the stories."

All the animals GASPED and stared at Anansi.

"I will do what you ask!" shouted Anansi.

All the animals laughed and laughed. How could feeble Anansi catch Mr Snake alive?

Anansi thought and thought and thought. He thought all day Monday.

Then on Tuesday he decided to build a rope trap. He made the rope trap with a strong vine from the banana tree. In the noose he laid Mr Snake's favourite food – mangoes! Mr Snake came slithering along. When he saw the mangoes he went CRUNCH! MUNCH! CRUNCH! MUNCH! CRUNCH! MUNCH!

Anansi pulled the rope trap and caught Mr Snake! But with one pull, heavy Mr Snake snapped the vine.

On Wednesday Anansi dug a deep hole in the ground and in it he put another of Mr Snake's favourite food – plantain! He made the sides slippery with grease then used his webbing to climb out of the hole. Anansi waited. Mr Snake came slithering along. When he saw the plantain he climbed into the hole and went CRUNCH! MUNCH! CRUNCH! MUNCH! CRUNCH! MUNCH!

Mr Snake then wrapped his tail around the trunk of a tree and pulled himself out.

On Thursday Anansi set a wooden cage above the bamboo tree. He then laid another of Mr Snake's favourite food under the cage – sweet potato! Anansi then waited high up in the tree.

Mr Snake came slithering along. When he saw the sweet potato he went CRUNCH! MUNCH! CRUNCH! MUNCH! CRUNCH! MUNCH!

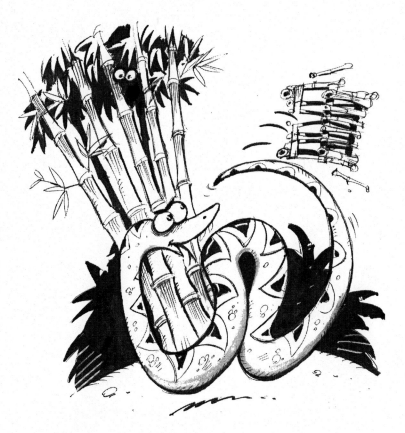

Anansi let go of the wooden cage and it landed on Mr Snake's head. But Mr Snake flicked it off with his strong tail.

Anansi thought and thought and thought. He thought all day Friday. But it was no use.

On Saturday Anansi saw Mr Snake resting by the river. "Good morning Mr Snake," said Anansi.

"*HOW DARE YOU!* I'm very angry with you Anansi!" said Mr Snake. "You've been trying to catch me all week! There was the rope trap on Tuesday, the hole on Wednesday and the cage on Thursday! *HOW DARE YOU!*"

"I'm sorry," said Anansi, "you are too clever. Now I can never prove to the other animals that you are the longest animal in the world, longer even than the bamboo tree."

"*HOW DARE YOU!* Of course I am longer than the bamboo tree! *HOW DARE YOU!* " hissed Mr Snake.

8

"I know that," said Anansi, "but all of the other animals said that you were not. I told them that you were and they all laughed at me."

"*HOW DARE THEY!* Cut down the bamboo tree and lay it next to me. I will prove I am longer! *HOW DARE THEY!*"

So Anansi cut down the bamboo tree and laid it next to Mr Snake.

Mr Snake slithered along until he was lined up with the bamboo tree.

"There!" said Mr Snake, "Now you can see that I am longer!"

Anansi walked up to Mr Snake's head and then down to Mr Snake's tail and then back up again.

"Mr Snake, you do appear to be longer than the bamboo tree. But how do I know that when I go up to look at your head you aren't crawling up and when I go down to look at your tail you aren't crawling down to make yourself look longer?"

"*HOW DARE YOU!* Of course I'm not cheating! Tie my head to the top of the bamboo tree with your webbing and then tie my tail to the bottom! You'll see then! I'll show you! I'll not be able to move then! *HOW DARE YOU!*" hissed Mr Snake.

So Anansi tied Mr Snake to the bamboo tree and called out, "Come here animals! Come here!"

All of the animals came out of the forest and saw Anansi standing next to Mr

Snake – he had caught Mr Snake alive! At
first they gasped but then they cheered and
shouted for Anansi. The animals soon fell
silent when Tiger arrived and saw Anansi
standing next to Mr Snake.

Tiger kept his promise and that is why, to this day, all of the stories in the Caribbean are called Anansi stories.

2: The Great Big Pussy Cat
(Norwegian)

There was once a woodcutter with his friend and his companion the great big brown bear walking through a forest. Now the woodcutter and the big brown bear made a fantastic team because the woodcutter would chop down the trees and the big brown bear would carry the sacks of logs over his great big shoulders.

On this particular day the woodcutter and the big brown bear had collected five sacks of logs. The big brown bear had two sacks over his great big shoulders and the woodcutter had one sack over his back.

But suddenly it began to snow. The snow came thick and fast and got deeper and deeper and deeper. The air around them got colder and colder and colder. It was so difficult to walk through the thick, deep snow that the woodcutter and the big brown bear dropped the sacks of logs. But even then it was still too difficult.

Just then, the woodcutter noticed a small cottage nearby. There were lights shining from the windows and smoke billowing out of the chimney; so the woodcutter knew someone was home. The woodcutter and the big brown bear trudged on through the thick, deep snow until they reached the front door of the cottage.

BANG! BANG! BANG! The woodcutter
knocked at the door.

A man named Eric answered the door.
"What do you want? Go away! Leave me
alone!" Eric said, sounding very frightened.

"Could we please take shelter from the snow in your cottage?" asked the woodcutter.

"No you can't! Go away! Leave me alone!" replied Eric.

"If you're frightened of my big brown bear, don't be, he's really very friendly," said the woodcutter.

"It's not that! Go away! Leave me alone!" Eric said again.

"Please don't turn us away," said the woodcutter, "we'll freeze to death out here!"

"I – I'm not trying to be mean," replied Eric, "it's just that . . . tomorrow is Sunday.

And Sunday . . . that's when the trolls come!"

"Trolls!" exclaimed the woodcutter. "We're more worried about the snow at the moment, please let us in."

Eric opened the door wide and into the cottage went the woodcutter and the big brown bear. They curled up on the rug by the fire and fell fast asleep.

They were awoken next morning by Eric and Eric's wife and children preparing a great big dinner. There was roast chicken, sausages, potatoes, vegetables and gravy, all sorts of good things to eat.

Eric and his family invited the woodcutter and the big brown bear to join them for their dinner but just as they all

sat down at the table there was suddenly a
BANG!!!

Out from down the chimney, out from
under the floorboards, out from the cracks
in the walls poured hundreds and hundreds
of trolls!

Some had big, long noses. Some had no noses at all.

Some had big, long tails. Some had no tails at all.

Some had big, long teeth. Some had no teeth at all.

But they were all ugly, they were all smelly and they were all ruining the dinner! Some jumped up and down on the roast chicken. Some played football with the potatoes. Some threw gravy up the windows. Some used the sausages like javelins.

Just then, the ugliest and the naughtiest of the trolls picked up a sausage from the table and walked right up to the big brown bear, "Here pussy, pussy, pussy!" it croaked.

"Would you like a sausage?"

Then it waved the sausage under the big brown bear's nose. The big brown bear licked his lips and reached out for the sausage.

But the troll snatched the sausage away screeching, "You can't have it pussy cat!"

Then the troll did it again! "Here pussy, pussy, pussy! Would you like a sausage?"

Again the big brown bear reached out for the sausage and again the troll snatched it away screeching, "You can't have it pussy cat!"

The troll did it over and over and over again.

The big brown bear got angrier and angrier and angrier, until he lifted up a great big brown paw and . . .
PHWPPPPPPPPPPPPPPPPPPT!

He squashed the troll flat!

Then the big brown bear ran all over the cottage squashing trolls as he went!

PHWPPPPPPPPPPPPPPPPPT!

PHWPPPPPPPPPPPPPPPPPT!

PHWPPPPPPPPPPPPPPPPPT!

PHWPPPPPPPPPPPPPPPPPT!

PHWPPPPPPPPPPPPPPPPPT!

The trolls all screamed, "Aaaaaaaargh!!!!" and jumped out of the window and ran off into the forest.

When every troll had gone the woodcutter picked up the mess from the floor, Eric and his family tidied the dinner table and the big brown bear licked the gravy from the windows.

When everything was set right they all sat down and ate together.

When they had finished the woodcutter noticed that it had stopped snowing outside. So he and the big brown bear said thank you to Eric and his family and went off into the forest collecting the sacks of logs as they went.

One week later, Eric and his family were just sitting down to their dinner when there was a loud BANG! BANG! BANG! at the door.

Eric opened the door and there in the doorway was an ugly little troll.

"Erm, I was just wondering," it croaked, "have you still got that big pussy cat that was here last week?"

"Oh, yes," answered Eric, "and she's had

kittens. Twelve of them! And they're all just as big as she is. Would you like to come in and meet them?"

"Oh no I wouldn't!" screeched the troll, "we're never coming in your house ever again!"

And off he ran into the forest.

From that day on Eric never saw a single troll ever again . . . all thanks to the woodcutter and the big brown bear that the trolls thought was a great big pussy cat.

3: The Lost Hammer
(Scandinavian)

The Thunder God was a mighty warrior. He carried a weapon called the Destroyer. The Destroyer was a hammer that had been made out of a meteorite that had crashed onto the Earth. An army of dwarves had made it into a weapon. It was so powerful that Thunder God could break the ice that covered the Earth in winter. So powerful that he could defeat whole armies with it. So powerful that he could throw it at any enemy and it would return to his hand in less than three seconds.

Thunder God lived with the other gods in a place called the City of Gods up in the clouds above the Earth. Thunder God's father was the king of all the gods which made Thunder God a god of great importance.

One morning, Thunder God woke up, scratched his armpits and looked around his bedroom. "WHERE'S MY HAMMER?!" he bellowed, "I'VE LOST MY HAMMER! WHERE'S MY HAMMER?!"

He looked under his bed and when it wasn't there, he threw his bed out of the window. "WHERE'S MY HAMMER?!" he bellowed again.

He looked behind his wardrobe and when it wasn't there, he threw his wardrobe out of the window.

"WHERE'S MY HAMMER?!" he bellowed once more.

He looked in his drawers and when it wasn't there, he threw his drawers out of the window.

Just then, Fire God was walking past Thunder God's house when he saw all of the bedroom furniture smashed all over the ground. Fire God went inside the house and up to Thunder God's bedroom.

"What ever's the matter?" asked Fire God.

"I'VE LOST MY HAMMER! WHERE'S MY HAMMER?!" bellowed Thunder God.

"You calm down," said Fire God, "you'll destroy the whole of the City of Gods at this rate. I'll find your hammer for you."

And with that Fire God changed himself into a bird and searched the whole of the City of Gods. When he couldn't find the hammer he flew down to the planet Earth and searched there too.

Eventually Fire God flew all the way to the City of Giants where all of the giants lived.

Fire God found the Giant King swimming in an icy lake just outside of the city. Fire God sat on a rock, then changed himself back into his normal form.

"Morning Giant King!" called Fire God cheerfully, "I'm looking for Thunder God's hammer. Have you seen it anywhere?"

"B-Wha! B-Wha! B-Wha!" laughed Giant King, "Yeah, I've nicked that 'ammer and you'll never find it 'cos I've 'idden it somewhere really good. B-Wha! B-Wha!

"Giant King, Thunder God will kill you when he finds out," warned Fire God.

"If any o'you gods come down here startin' trouble and you kill me then you'll never find that 'ammer," boomed Giant King.

Fire God rubbed his chin, smiled and said, "Giant King, you really are a clever giant. There must be something you want in return for the hammer."

Giant King scratched the back of his large, bald head and said, "Well, there is this goddess that lives up in the City of Gods and I've 'eard she's gorgeous. If she agrees to be my wife, then I'll give the 'ammer as a wedding gift."

Fire God looked horrified, "Giant King,

you're talking about the Love Goddess! I don't mean to be rude but she is a beautiful goddess and you have a wart on your nose the size of a beach ball. I don't think she'll marry you."

"Either she agrees to be my wife or you don't get your 'ammer back!!! Awright?!" bellowed Giant King.

Fire God changed himself back into a bird and flew to the City of Gods. Once there he went to see Love Goddess and explained it all to her.

"I'm not marrying that big ugly giant!" she screeched. "He has a wart on his nose the size of a beach ball and any way I'm already married. Get lost Fire God!"

Fire God went to see King God.

"What will we do Fire God?" asked King God. "We need that hammer to break the ice on Earth in the winter. Without it the Earth will freeze over completely and all of the humans will die!"

"Well my king, I do have one idea, but please hear me out on this," said Fire God with a smile on his face. "How about we put a little lipstick on Thunder God. Perhaps a little eyeliner and a pretty dress. We could pretend he is Love Goddess and when the wedding ceremony is over Thunder God can take the hammer back!"

"My son won't like this!" laughed King God.

And sure enough when Thunder God heard of Fire God's plan he boomed, "I'M NOT DRESSING UP LIKE A WOMAN!"

But King God was his father and the king of the gods and when King God insisted – he meant it! So Thunder God was put in a pretty dress, given some lipstick and some eyeliner and was magically transformed into Love Goddess, the goddess of love and beauty.

"THIS IS NEVER GOING TO WORK!" boomed Thunder God.

Fire God and Thunder God travelled down to the Earth and into the City of Giants.

All of the giants were gathered on a field for the ceremony. When Giant King saw Thunder God, he looked at the pretty dress, he looked at the lipstick, he looked at the eyeliner, he looked at the beard then he

34

said, "Ooooh, she's gorgeous! Let's get married straight away!"

"I WANT MY WEDDING PRESENT BEFORE I MARRY YOU," bellowed Thunder God.

Giant King nodded to his servants excitedly and the hammer was brought forward on a purple velvet cushion. Thunder God took that hammer in one hand and with the other he wiped off the lipstick, wiped off the eyeliner and pulled off the dress.

"AHA!" he boomed, "I AM THUNDER GOD AND I HAVE FOOLED YOU ALL!"

Then Thunder God killed every last giant on Earth.

Thunder God and Fire God returned to the City of Gods and nobody was ever allowed to talk about the time that Thunder God dressed up like a woman. Although Fire God did occasionally call him . . . Thunder Goddess.

4: Ching Ping and the Dragon
(Chinese)

Ching Ping was a woodcutter. But not any
kind of woodcutter. Ching Ping was the best
woodcutter the land had ever seen, all
thanks to his golden axe. The golden axe
could cut through wood like it was butter.
And Ching Ping could fill his wheelbarrow in
no time at all.

But the problem was that the forest
that Ching Ping lived near, was getting
smaller and smaller and smaller.

Ching Ping and his wife, Mina, decided to move on and find a new village to live in, with a bigger forest. So they packed up all of their possessions, including the golden axe, and set off. They were sad about leaving, but knew that it was the best thing to do to save the forest.

In those days you could not get a plane, train or car to get to where you wanted to go, Ching Ping and Mina had to walk, leading their mule carrying all their possessions.

When they arrived at the village they walked down the busy street and into the busy inn and asked the innkeeper if the village needed a woodcutter.

"No," replied the innkeeper, "we already have a woodcutter in this village."

So Ching Ping and Mina set up their tent and spent the night just outside of the village.

The following day they set off again towards the next village and after a whole day of travelling they arrived.

They walked down the busy street and into the busy inn and asked the innkeeper if the village needed a woodcutter.

"No," replied the innkeeper, "we already have a woodcutter in this village."

So Ching Ping and Mina set up their tent and spent the night just outside of this village. The following day they set off towards the next village and when they got there can you guess what happened? . . .

The innkeeper told Ching Ping and Mina that they already had a woodcutter. The same thing happened every day for three weeks. One village a day, twenty-one villages in all.

When they arrived at the twenty-second village something was different.

Ching Ping and Mina walked down the quiet, deserted street and into the quiet, deserted inn. There was no one to be seen.

"Where is everybody?" asked Mina.

"I don't know," said Ching Ping. He knocked on the wooden bar and called out, "Hello! Is there anybody there?"

No reply.

So Ching Ping knocked harder this time and called out louder, "Hello! Is there anybody there?"

But there was still no reply.

"Why don't you ring that bell on the bar, Ching Ping? Maybe that's what it's for," said Mina.

So Ching Ping rang the bell and called, "Hello! Is there anybody there?"

A trap door behind the bar opened very slowly and two beady eyes and a long crooked nose peered out. "What do you want?" the beady eyes and crooked nose asked very quickly and very gruffly.

"Erm, well, I was wondering if you could help me, my name is Ching Ping and this is - "

"Go away!" shouted the beady eyes and crooked nose, then the trap door slammed shut.

"How rude!" exclaimed Mina.

Ching Ping rang the bell again and called, "Hello! Is there anybody there?"

"What do you want?" the beady eyes and crooked nose snapped again.

"Please come up and talk to us," said Ching Ping, "we won't hurt you."

The trap door swung open and the grumpy innkeeper with the two beady eyes and long crooked nose climbed out and stood behind the wooden bar nervously.

"I was wondering if your village needed a woodcutter?" asked Ching Ping.

"A woodcutter? A woodcutter, you say? Yes we do!" replied the innkeeper sharply. "But nobody . . . nobody wants to go into the forest around here."

"But why?" asked Mina.

"Because in this forest there lurks . . . a big, horrible, green, scaly . . . dragon!"

"A dragon!" exclaimed Ching Ping and Mina together.

"Yes, but if you're brave enough to go into the forest and get some wood, then the job is yours. Until then go away!" said the innkeeper and then hurried off back into the cellar, slamming the trap door shut behind him.

"What do you think?" asked Mina.

"I think he's mad. I don't believe in dragons. I'll go into the forest and use my golden axe. I'll be back in no time at all," replied Ching Ping.

So Ching Ping unpacked his golden axe, then he got his wheelbarrow from the mules back and set off into the forest. He walked through the quiet, deserted streets into the deep, dark forest. When Ching Ping reached a clearing in the middle of the forest he set down his wheelbarrow next to a tree and he began swinging the golden axe, which made a

WHOOOSH sound on every stroke.

WHOOOSH, WHOOOSH, WHOOOSH.

And in no time at all, the wheelbarrow was nearly full.

But, Ching Ping began to feel very tired. So he stopped for a rest.

Just then, Ching Ping started to hear another sound faintly in the distance. He began to listen. Boom, Boom, Boom, the sound went.

Then it got louder . . .
Boom! Boom! Boom!
Then even louder . . .
Boom! Boom! Boom!

Ching Ping began to get nervous so he decided to head back to the inn. But now the sound was so loud that Ching Ping could not work out which direction it was coming from! If he ran, he could run into whatever was making the loud, booming noise.

Boom! Boom! Boom! the sound went. Then even louder . . .
Boom! Boom! Boom!

Ching Ping started turning in circles looking for where the sound was coming from. Then suddenly the sound stopped . . . Ching Ping heard a different sound. This sound was deep, heavy breathing. It came from behind Ching Ping. He started to turn around to look behind him.

As he turned round, he was confronted by something terrifying!

There, standing in front of him, was a big, horrible, green, scaly . . . dragon! It had two red eyes, long white teeth and its huge wings stretched out across the forest clearing.

The dragon stared at Ching Ping below him and took in a long, deep, breath, then slowly began to lower his head towards Ching Ping.

Its hot, smelly breath snorted into Ching Ping's face as its mouth got wider and wider and wider still.

The dragon took another long deep breath . . . and then suddenly he said, "Oh, I'm terribly sorry to bother you but could you help me?" in a voice that sounded just like the Queen of England's.

"W-W-What?" stuttered Ching Ping.

"Well I was wondering if you could help me," continued the dragon, very politely, "you see I'm rather lost and in need of some directions. Do you know these parts well?"

"S-So you're not going to eat me then?" asked Ching Ping.

"Eat you?! Oh, goodness me, no! I'm a vegetarian! I only eat fruit and vegetables!" replied the dragon.

"Wh-where do you want to go?" Ching Ping managed to blurt out, still a little petrified.

"I'm looking for the Rocky Mountains. I was meant to be at a dragon party there about a week ago, but I'm useless with directions. I tried asking some of those lovely people in the village but they all seemed to be in a dreadful hurry themselves and when I've been back there, no one has been around at all. Can you help me?" explained the dragon.

"Oh . . . erm . . . right then," said Ching Ping, a lot less nervous now, "the Rocky Mountains, right, well you need to head east towards the sun, that way, and you can't miss them."

"Ah, I see. Oh, well thank you so much. What's your name?" asked the dragon.

"Ching Ping."

"Well my name is Drago. Thanks awfully for your help Ching Ping. Ta-ta for now." Then Drago spread his huge wings and flew off into the distance.

Ching Ping picked up his golden axe and wheelbarrow and then ran as fast as he could back to the village inn.

"Oh, I was so worried, are you alright?" asked Mina.

"Yes, but you'll never believe what happened!" said Ching Ping.

Just then the innkeeper with the two beady eyes and long crooked nose quickly climbed out of the cellar and stood behind the wooden bar, but before Ching Ping could explain what had happened, the innkeeper began ringing the bell from behind the bar furiously and ran out into street shouting, "Hoorah for Ching Ping, he's rid the village of the horrible monster! Hoorah!"

Ching Ping and Mina followed him and saw all of the villagers cautiously stepping out into the street.

Ching Ping began trying to explain what had happened, but the villagers had picked him up onto their shoulders and began carrying him through the village shouting, "Ching Ping! Ching Ping! Ching Ping! Hooray!"

So Ching Ping and Mina were offered a job and a home in the village for as long as they wanted.

They tried to explain to everyone what really happened in the forest many times, but nobody would believe them, after all, whoever heard of a vegetarian dragon?

5: How the Giraffe Got his Long Neck
(African)

A long, long, long, long, long, long, long, long, long, long, long, long, long time ago, there lived a giraffe in Africa. That long ago, the giraffe looked very different from the way he looks today because instead of having a great long neck, this giraffe had a tiny, little neck.

All of the food that Giraffe liked was in the tall, tall trees and Giraffe was just too short to reach them. Giraffe was feeling really hungry, so he went across the African plain to find out what his friends were eating.

The first animal that he came across was Lion.

"Lion!" said Giraffe, "I'm soooooooooo hungry. What are you eating?"

"I'm eating MEAT!" roared Lion.

"Bluuuuuurgh!!!" said Giraffe, "you're eating meat? I don't want any meat. I'll go and find someone else."

So Giraffe went across the African plain until he came across Zebra.

"Zebra!" said Giraffe, "I'm soooooooooo hungry. What are you eating?"

"I'm eating GRASS," chewed Zebra.

"Bluuuuuurgh!!!" said Giraffe, "you're eating grass? I don't want any grass. I'll go and find someone else."

So Giraffe went across the African plain until he came across Snake.

"Snake!" said Giraffe, "I'm soooooooooo hungry. What are you eating?"

"I'm eating VOLESSSSSSSSS," hissed Snake.

"Bluuuuuurgh!!!" said Giraffe, "you're eating voles? I don't even know what they are, so I certainly don't want any voles. I'll go and find someone else."

So Giraffe went across the African plain until he came across Hyena.

"Hyena!" said Giraffe, "I'm sooooooooo hungry. What are you eating?"

"HA! HA! I'm eating DEAD THINGS," laughed Hyena.

"Bluuuuuurgh!!!" said Giraffe, "you're eating dead things? I don't want any dead things. I know, I'll go and find Mouse. He's a sensible animal."

So Giraffe went across the African plain until he came across the place where Mouse lived.

Now Mouse lived in a hole underground next to a tall, tall tree.

Giraffe peered into the hole and called, "Hello Mouse!" But there was no answer so he peered a bit further into the hole and called, "Hello Mouse!!!"

But there was no answer so he put his head further inside the hole and called, "Hello Mouse!!!"

Giraffe realised that Mouse wasn't home but when he went to take his head out of the hole, he realised it was stuck!

Just then Mouse came home and he could see Giraffe with his head in the hole and his bottom in the air.

Mouse squeaked, "Erm, Giraffe, what are you doing with your head in my home?"

"I'm stuck!" screamed Giraffe. "Help me!"

Mouse went around the back, grabbed hold of Giraffe's tail and he pulled and pulled and pulled.

But it was no good, he couldn't get Giraffe out of the hole. Mouse decided to go and get some help.

He went across the African plain until he came across Hyena.

"Hyena," squeaked Mouse, "could you help me get Giraffe out of my home please?"

"HA! HA! Of course I can!" laughed Hyena and the animals went across the African plain until they came to Giraffe.

When they got there, Mouse grabbed hold of Giraffe's tail, Hyena grabbed hold of Mouse's tail and they pulled and pulled and pulled.

But it was no good, they couldn't get Giraffe out of the hole. So they went back across the African plain until they came across Snake.

"Snake," squeaked Mouse, "could you help me get Giraffe out of my home please?"

"Of coursssssssse I can!" hissed Snake and the animals went across the African plain until they came to Giraffe.

When they got there, Mouse grabbed hold of Giraffe's tail, Hyena grabbed hold of Mouse's tail, Snake grabbed hold of Hyena's tail and they pulled and pulled and pulled.

But it was no good, they still couldn't get Giraffe out of the hole. So they went back across the African plain until they came across Zebra.

"Zebra," squeaked Mouse, "could you help me get Giraffe out of my home please?"

"Of course I can!" chewed Zebra and the animals went across the African plain until they came to Giraffe.

When they got there, Mouse grabbed hold of Giraffe's tail, Hyena grabbed hold of Mouse's tail, Snake grabbed hold of Hyena's tail, Zebra grabbed hold of Snake's tail and they pulled and pulled and pulled.
But it was no good, they still couldn't get Giraffe out of the hole.

So back they went across the African plain until they came across Lion.

"Lion," squeaked Mouse, "could you help me get Giraffe out of my home please?"

"Of course I can!" roared Lion and the animals went across the African plain until they came to Giraffe.

When they got there, Mouse grabbed hold of Giraffe's tail, Hyena grabbed hold of Mouse's tail, Snake grabbed hold of Hyena's tail, Zebra grabbed hold of Snake's tail, Lion was tempted to bite Zebra, but he didn't, he only grabbed hold of his tail. Then they all pulled together and they all pulled together and they all pulled together.

Then POP!!!! out of the hole came Giraffe's head.

All of the animals landed in a heap on top of each other. The first animal to get to his feet was Giraffe.

"Oh, thank you my friends, thank you so much for helping . . . me . . . "

Giraffe realised that all of his friends were a VERY long way down.

"Look at my neck!" he screamed. "It's massive!"

Then he ran around in circles screaming, "Look at my neck! Look at my neck! Look at my neck! Look at my neck! Look at my neck!" Just then Giraffe noticed that the tall, tall tree next to Mouse's hole was just at eye level. So he had a little nibble at the leaves in that tree. Then he had another nibble. Then he had a bigger nibble. Then he ate every single leaf in that tree until he was nice and full.

Giraffe never went hungry again. And that is why, to this day, giraffes have really long necks.

6: Jack and the Squirrel
(Scottish)

Jack was in the forest collecting firewood and he had spent the whole morning cheerfully filling his sack. He stopped for a rest but as he did so, he suddenly saw something go VOOOOOOOOOOOOOOOM!!! across the forest floor from behind one tree to another.

Jack had never seen anything move so quickly and he decided to see what it was. But as soon as he got close . . .

VOOOOOOOOOOOOOOOM!!! Off it went again behind another tree.

Jack chased after it, but as soon as he got close . . . VOOOOOOOOOOOOOOOM!!! and VOOOOOOOOOOOOOOOM!!! and VOOOOOOOOOOOOOOOM!!! again!

Then Jack had an idea. He had made himself some peanut butter sandwiches for his lunch that day. So he unwrapped a sandwich, knelt down on the floor and held it out in his hands in front of him.

Out from behind the closest tree hopped a tiny, cute, bushy tailed . . . pink squirrel.

The squirrel looked at Jack cautiously. Then blinked twice and hopped into Jack's hand.

With a CRUNCH, MUNCH! CRUNCH,
MUNCH! CRUNCH, MUNCH! The squirrel ate
all of the sandwich and then looked up at
Jack with its big brown eyes. And Jack
looked at its big bushy tail,

"That's the cutest thing I've ever seen!"
said Jack, "I'll take him home and keep him
for a pet. Lorna will love him!"

Just then a loud, thumping sound echoed through the forest.

BANG! BANG! BANG! went the sound as it got nearer.

The squirrel became so frightened that it jumped into Jack's jacket and quivered.

Jack gathered his firewood and began heading home as quickly as he could, but the thumping noise was getting louder and louder.

BANG! BANG! BANG!

Jack realised that he could not outrun whatever it was, so he hid behind a large bush and peered into the forest towards the sound of the loud, thumping noise.

Through a clearing in the forest Jack and the squirrel could see what was making the loud, thumping noise.

There heading right towards them making a deafening BANG!!! with each footstep was an enormous giant! The giant stopped, sniffed the air and then stomped away through the forest with deafening footsteps.

When all was quiet again, Jack lifted the squirrel from his jacket, held him in his hands and carefully carried him to his home. He told his wife, Lorna, all about what had happened in the forest. The squirrel looked up at Lorna with its big brown eyes and Lorna looked at its big bushy tail, "That's the cutest thing I've ever seen!" said Lorna. The squirrel blinked twice at her and then hopped from Jack's hand to Lorna's hand.

Jack made a huge plate of peanut butter sandwiches and the squirrel ate the lot with a CRUNCH, MUNCH! CRUNCH, MUNCH! CRUNCH, MUNCH!

Then Jack and Lorna laid a soft cushion by the fire and watched as the squirrel drifted off to sleep. They went to bed that night feeling very happy with their new pet and slept peacefully in their beds until . . .

CRASH!!!

Jack and Lorna leapt out of their beds. Their whole roof had been ripped off! They could see the night sky above them. And then they could see an enormous, a gigantic, a massive hand reaching into the cottage! It was the giant!

Just then Lorna realised that the hand was reaching to grab the squirrel.

"NOOO!" she shouted and ran forward to stop the giant but the huge hand swatted her away like a fly. Lorna hit the floor with a thud.

"NOOO!" shouted Jack as he ran forward to stop the giant but the huge hand swatted him away like a fly too.

The giant lowered his hand inside the cottage towards the squirrel getting closer and closer and closer. It reached out a long finger and poked the squirrel.

"TAG! You're it! Hee! Hee! Hee!" boomed the giant and with a BANG! BANG! BANG! skipped off into the forest.

The squirrel sat up, shrugged its shoulders and hopped off chasing the giant.

Jack and Lorna looked at their bumps and their bruises. They looked at the hole in their roof and they decided never again to take in any of the woodland creatures from the forest, as it really wasn't worth it.

7: The Fairies of Rothley Mill

(English)

There was once a boy named Ralph who lived at Rothley Mill. He was the son of a miller but he never helped his father. He preferred spending his days hurting little creatures in the wood or stealing eggs from the hen house just to smash them or chasing the field mice with sticks. He was a bully. And like all bullies, he was only cruel to things that were smaller than him and could not fight for themselves.

Every evening, if the weather was fine, he would sit on top of an old kiln near the mill and throw stones at a squirrel that lived nearby. He kept a pocket full of large flat stones and he would chuckle to himself as he sat on the mill waiting for the squirrel. "Huh! Huh! Huh!"

One evening Ralph heard a noise unlike any other he had heard before. It was like the tinkling of lots of little bells all chiming together.

As the sound drew nearer and louder, Ralph lay down on the kiln and hid because, like all bullies, he was easily frightened. Ralph saw, getting nearer and nearer, a whole procession of fairies! They were no bigger than daffodils and wore sycamore that shone in the setting sun. Each rode a miniature horse and from the harnesses hung little bells, each chiming a pretty sound. It was this chiming that Ralph could hear.

Ralph watched them with wide eyes as he lay flatter on the roof. He had never seen fairies before. He saw them dismount, tie their horses to bullrushes and go into the kiln. From a spy hole on top of the kiln Ralph watched as the fairies lit a little fire with fir cones and twigs. Then they filled a miniature cauldron and began to make porridge. Once the porridge bubbled, they each took an acorn cup, dipped it into the cauldron and began their tiny feast.

After eating, they danced and sang around the fire.

"La, la, la, la, la, laaaaaaaaaaaaaaaaaaaaaa!"

It was a beautiful sight to see them
throwing their golden hair as they danced
and sang.

But Ralph soon began to think about how he could hurt the fairies. He thought it would be so funny to interrupt their party with a real scare. At last he decided to use one of the large, flat stones he kept in his pocket for throwing at the squirrels. He carefully aimed and dropped the stone into the spy hole. He slapped his hand over his mouth as it landed on the cauldron and the fire, scattering hot porridge and fiery embers in all directions.

He bellowed with laughter "Huh! Huh! Huh!"

But he soon stopped laughing when he saw a hundred pairs of little eyes looking at him. And a hundred little fingers pointing at him.

"Burnt and scalded!" they chanted. "Burnt and scalded!"

Their little voices were filled with such ferocity that Ralph became frightened and jumped off the kiln and decided to get home as quickly as he could.

He began to run across the field towards his home, but the fairies leapt onto their horses and galloped after him chanting "Burnt and scalded!" over and over again.

Ralph kept looking round at the fairies as they got closer and closer.

"Burnt and scalded! Burnt and scalded! Burnt and scalded! Burnt and scalded!"

Just then Ralph tripped on the long grass and before he could get up the fairies leapt onto his leg chanting, "Burnt and scalded! Burnt and scalded! Burnt and scalded! Burnt and scalded!"

They tore and scratched at Ralph's leg, but he soon managed to shake them off and ran home weeping and wailing. When he got home Ralph checked his leg and there wasn't a scratch on him.

"Stupid fairies!" laughed Ralph, "They didn't scare me. Just wait until I get one of them on their own! Huh! Huh! Huh!"

Ralph went to bed early. But in the middle of the night he felt a terrible pain all over his leg.

A burning pain. A scalding pain.
He pulled off the bed sheets and saw that his leg was blackened and scarred. His leg had been burnt and scalded!

"I'm sorry! I'm so very sorry!" shouted Ralph. "Oh I'm so sorry for all of the things I've done! And I promise never to hurt anything ever again!"

Through his tears Ralph watched as his leg returned to normal. He kept his promise too and he never ever hurt anything again.

8: Black Pepper
(English)

I always carry a bottle of black pepper around with me. Why? Well it all started when I was in the playground with my mate Nick. Now Nick and I, we were always getting up to the stupidest of things. I remember Nick said to me, "Here, did you know that if you were to sneeze with your eyes open, your eyes go shooting out of your head!"

"Cool!" I said, "Shall we try it?"

We spent that playtime trying to make each other sneeze. We tickled each other's chins, we tickled each other's noses, we even tried shoving dandelion seeds up each other's nostrils. But no matter how hard we tried we just couldn't sneeze.

While I was shoving a particularly large seed up Nick's nostrils, I suddenly heard a booming voice from behind me, "What on earth are you two doin'?"

It was Greg Cook the school bully. Greg Cook who hated Nick and I. Everyone called him Cooky.

"We're not doing anything Cooky," I said.

Cooky shoved us both to the ground and kicked us before he walked off laughing.

"I'm sick of this," I said, "I'm going to go and tell the teacher."

We went straight into Mr Blackford's class and I said, "Mr Blackford – "

But Mr Blackford didn't even look up from the work on his desk. He put his hand straight out and said, "Homework."

"Homework? Homework?! Homework!!!" I thought.

I had forgotten to do my homework and so had Nick. Mr Blackford gave us five extra sheets to do that night as a punishment.

We walked home from school feeling miserable. We had been kicked by the school bully and given five sheets of homework to do as a punishment. We were not happy. Nick went off to his house and I went into mine. I decided to get on with my homework straight away so that I could watch the Simpsons later on. But as I sat down with my sheets laid out in front of me, my mind began to wander onto other things.

I thought about what Nick had said, 'If you sneeze with your eyes open, your eyes go shooting out of your head!' I wondered if it was true?

So I went into the kitchen and got myself a bottle of black pepper. I walked into the living room and unscrewed the cap. As soon as I did I started sneezing all over the place.

AACHOO!!! AACHOO!!! AACHOO!!! AACHOO!!!

But no matter how hard I tried, I just couldn't keep my eyes open. I was about to give up when I decided to give it one last go.

I stared at the floor. I sniffed the black pepper. I sneezed, AAACCHHOOOO!!!!!

and I kept my eyes open, but my eyes didn't go shooting out of my head. Something very strange happened though.

I suddenly began floating in the air. The top of my head touched the ceiling. I stayed there for a few moments and then I gently drifted back to the ground.

"Wooooaaah!" I said to myself, "I've got to try this outside!" I ran to the garden and stood on the lawn. I stared at the floor. I sniffed the black pepper. I sneezed, AAAAACCHHOOOOO!!!!!

I kept my eyes open and again up into the air I went! About six metres up! I could see over all of the next door neighbours' fences. I could see Tiddles the neighbour's cat.

"Hello Tiddles!" I said, but Tiddles just ran away scared.

I stayed there for a few moments, floating, levitating, hovering. Then I gently drifted to the ground.

I was about to try it again when I suddenly heard my mum shouting, "Adam, have you finished your homework yet?"

I went inside and did my homework but it took me all night, I couldn't stop thinking about the black pepper. But in the morning, when the doorbell rang I went running downstairs and there was Nick.

"You'll never guess what!!!" I said.

"You'll never guess what," he answered, "I've not done my homework again."

We had to walk to school so slowly because Nick was filling in his homework sheets that we didn't have any time in the playground, we had to go straight into lessons.

I sat there in Mr Blackford's class willing it to be playtime. And eventually it was. The bell rang and we all ran outside.

I stood in the middle of the playground.

"Hey, everybody! Watch this!" I called. A crowd gathered around me.

I took the black pepper from my pocket.

I stared at the floor. I sniffed, I sneezed, AAAAACCHHOOOOO!!!!!

I kept my eyes open but at that exact moment I heard that familiar voice behind me again,

"What are you losers doin' now?"

It was Cooky!

I floated up into the air, I turned my body around to face him and with the deepest, most booming voice I had I said, "LEAVE – US – ALONE!"

Cooky screamed and ran off into the toilets. Cooky never bothered us again, but that is why I always carry a bottle of black pepper with me, because you never know when you might need it.

9: Follow Up Activities for Teachers

Storytelling that leads to Story Writing in four Simple Steps

Step One - Anansi the Storyteller/ The Great Big Pussy Cat

These stories can be followed up by asking the children what their favourite part of the story was and writing it on the board. Once all of the favourite parts are listed the children should be asked to work in pairs.

In their pairs they should be given a large sheet of paper and asked to make a 'Story Map'. This means that they have to write in note form or even draw pictures to retell the story. However, they must try and list the main events in chronological order and link each event with an arrow.

Once the Story Maps are completed ask the children to join a different pair and the two groups show each other their maps. Do they notice anything different? Do they need to add anything to their own Story Map?

The children are then going to work in their original pairs again. This activity is called 'Tag Team Storytelling'. One of the pair starts to retell the story. They are to have a last, lingering look at the Story Map to help before they start, but after that all of the Story Maps are to be collected and the board wiped. They then orally tell their partner the story from the beginning. If they get stuck, they can 'tag' their partner to take over. If their partner gets stuck later on they too can 'tag' and so on.

Once the story has been told they swap so that the other person starts the story and again they can continue to 'tag' each other to help them remember.

'Tag Team Storytelling' will catch on fast and can be used for any story and can dramatically help speaking and listening.

Step Two - The Lost Hammer/ Ching Ping and The Dragon

These stories can be used to assist the children with their story ideas. Ask the children what happened in the story. They should try to orally identify the key features. Make notes of these

For example in the 'Ching Ping and the Dragon' story the key features could be:

1. Ching Ping and his wife Mina need to find a new village to live in.
2. They try lots of villages but no-one needs a woodcutter.
3. They come to an abandoned village and meet a grumpy innkeeper who tells them about a dragon in the forest.
4. Ching Ping goes to the forest and hears a BOOM! BOOM! BOOM!
5. The dragon scares Ching Ping.
6. The dragon turns out to be friendly, Ching Ping and Mina become the woodcutters of the village.

Give the children a comic strip grid with, in this case, six boxes on the sheet. Ask the children to draw six simple illustrations for the six key features of the story. This storyboard will help the children remember the story if they wish to retell it.

The children are then going to change three key features of the story.

First, ask the children to change the dragon into another creature, e.g. a lion, a dinosaur, a ghost etc.

Secondly, the children should change the main characters of the story from Ching Ping and Mina to any other story character, such as Jack from Jack and the Beanstalk or Red Riding Hood from Little Red Riding Hood. Or perhaps they could now be the main characters so that the story becomes in the first person.

Finally, change the grumpy innkeeper to another character, e.g. a friendly innkeeper, a scared troll, a rich king.

Next, the children should name their new story so instead of 'Ching Ping and the Dragon' it could now be 'Jack and the Lion' or 'Red Riding Hood and the Dinosaur' or 'Adam and the Ghost'.

The children can then make a new storyboard of their own story and use it to help them tell this story. This storyboard can also be used to help them write their story too.

Step Three - How the Giraffe Got his Long Neck/Jack and the Squirrel

These stories can be followed up by asking the children to think about the common patterns in the stories, such as in the 'How the Giraffe Got

His Long Neck' there is a lot of repetition, it happened a long time ago, the story ends with a problem being solved, the story ends with the animals looking like they do today, the story also ends with the story title, etc.

Using this story as an example, the children should choose their favourite animal. Then they should think about the most distinguishing feature of that animal, e.g. If they choose a rhino it may be the rhino's horn, or a shark's teeth or a hyena's laugh.

Next the children should think about a good story title for their animal, e.g. How The Rhino Got its Horn, How The Shark Got its Sharp Teeth, How The Hyena Got Its Laugh.

The children should then be asked to get into groups of 3, 4 or 5 in mixed ability. They should tell each other what their story title is. The group votes on which story title they would like to work on.

After that the group should try and make a story plan for what could happen to their animal. For example a rough storyline could be:

BEGINNING – The hyena was always grumpy and

never ever laughed. The other animals felt sorry for him.

MIDDLE – All of the animals take turns in trying to make the hyena laugh.

END – The clown fish (or any other animal) makes the hyena laugh and he has never stopped laughing. That is how the hyena got his laugh.

Once the group has a rough story plan they present it to the rest of the class.

The children then individually work on their own story using ideas either from their group or one that they have heard from another group.
The best way to present this kind of story is either using a comic strip or a picture book. The children could then read or tell orally their story to younger children in the school.

Step Four - The Fairies of Rothley Mill/Black Pepper

These stories can be used to assist the children with their short story writing. Ask the children to identify what they like about the stories. One of the key features may be that they were surprised by what happened. The unexpected part of a story is what makes it work.

The children should be placed in mixed ability groups of 3, 4 or 5 and then given a choice of four story starters. They choose which story starter they wish to work on and it is their job to make up the rest of the story. But, they must put in a twist in the tale, something the reader would not expect to happen.

Any four story starters will work but here are some examples:

STORY STARTER ONE - A boy or a girl decide they want super powers like Spiderman. He/she went to the zoo to get bitten by a spider. But they were bitten by a different animal and now he/she has the power of that animal . . .

STORY STARTER TWO - A group of friends were playing football when they kicked the ball down a well. One of the friends peered inside the well and beside the football they saw something unusual. Something was shining . . .

STORY STARTER THREE - A boy or a girl was on his/her way home from school when he/she passes a deserted house. They saw lights flashing in an upstairs window. He/she rushed to tell his/her friends . . .

STORY STARTER FOUR – A group of friends were on a farm when they heard strange noises coming from an abandoned barn. They decided to investigate. When they opened the barn door it was dark and they stepped inside . . .

The children should then make a story plan for the rest of the story using notes or sentences or pictures to create ideas. Once the group has a rough story plan they present it to the rest of the class.

After that the children individually work on their own story using ideas either from their group or one that they have heard from another group. With the confidence they have gained from the former three steps the children could then write their ideas up as a short story.

Also available in the Reluctant Reader Series from:

PUBLISHING

Grandma's Teeth *(Humorous)*
David Webb   ISBN 978 1 905637 20 1

Trevor's Trousers *(Humorous)*
David Webb   ISBN 978 1 904904 19

The Library Ghost *(Mystery)*
David Webb   ISBN 978 1 904374 66

Dinosaur Day *(Adventure)*
David Webb   ISBN 978 1 904374 67 1

Chip McGraw *(Cowboy Mystery)*
Ian MacDonald   ISBN 978 1 905637 08 9

Eyeball Soup *(Science Fiction)*
Ian MacDonald   ISBN 978 1 904904 59 5

Close Call *(Mystery - Interest age 12+)*
Sandra Glover   ISBN 978 1 905 637 07 2

Deadline *(Adventure)*
Sandra Glover   ISBN 978 1 904904 30 4

Cracking Up *(Humorous)*
Sandra Glover   ISBN 978 1 904904 86 1

Beastly Things in the Barn *(Humorous)*
Sandra Glover   ISBN 978 1 904904 96 0
www.sandraglover.co.uk

The Owlers *(Adventure)*
Stephanie Baudet   ISBN 978 1 904904 87 8

The Curse of the Full Moon *(Mystery)*
Stephanie Baudet   ISBN 978 1 904904 11 3

The Haunted Windmill *(Mystery)*
Margaret Nash   ISBN 978 1 904904 22 9

Order online @ **www.eprint.co.uk**